Ladybird Readers

Superhero Max

Series Editor: Sorrel Pitts
Text adapted by Sorrel Pitts
Illustrated by Ed Myer

LADYBIRD BOOKS

UK | USA | Canada | Ireland | Australia
India | New Zealand | South Africa

Ladybird Books is part of the Penguin Random House group of companies
whose addresses can be found at global.penguinrandomhouse.com
www.penguin.co.uk   www.puffin.co.uk   www.ladybird.co.uk

Penguin
Random House
UK

First published 2017
001

Copyright © Ladybird Books Ltd, 2017

The moral rights of the author and illustrator have been asserted.

Printed in China

A CIP catalogue record for this book is available from the British Library

ISBN: 978-0-241-28368-4

All correspondence to:
Ladybird Books
Penguin Random House Children's
80 Strand, London WC2R 0RL

MIX
Paper from
responsible sources
FSC® C018179

Superhero Max

Picture words

Superhero Max

rob

(verb)

magic boots

Lady Rob   Ricky Rob

policeman

Max was a boy. He was a superhero, too.

Max had magic boots. He wore the boots, and he was Superhero Max!

Superhero Max stopped bad people, and he helped good people.

Ricky Rob was a bad person.
He robbed banks.

Lady Rob was Ricky's mom,
and she was a bad person, too.

She liked robbing banks
with Ricky.

9

Lady Rob liked playing bad games with people.

"Help me!" she said. "I cannot open my door!"

Superhero Max flew to her house and opened the door.

"Thank you, Superhero Max!" said Lady Rob. "Would you like some tea?"

Superhero Max had some tea. But it was magic tea, and soon he slept.

Lady Rob took Superhero Max's magic boots!

13

"I want the magic boots, Mom," said Ricky Rob. "Then, I can rob the bank!"

"No!" said Lady Rob. "I want to rob the bank!"

"One, two, fly!" said Lady Rob, and she flew above the houses.

15

A boy ran to Superhero Max.

"You must not sleep," he said. "Lady Rob wants to rob the bank!"

"I can help!" said Superhero Max.

But he did not have any magic boots. He could not fly!

Superhero Max ran to
the bank.

"Lady Rob! Stop!" he said.

But Lady Rob was in
the bank!

Lady Rob ran from the bank with all the money.

"You cannot fly, Superhero Max!" she said.

Lady Rob and Ricky Rob
flew above the houses.
They had the money from
the bank!

"You cannot stop us,
Superhero Max!" they said.

"But I can stop the magic boots," said Superhero Max.

Superhero Max sent magic to the boots. The boots and the bad people flew to a policeman.

"We caught you, Lady Rob! We caught you, Ricky Rob!" said Superhero Max. "You cannot rob the bank again."

"Thank you, Superhero Max!" said the policeman. "You ARE a superhero!"

Soon, Max was back in his house.

"Help, Superhero Max! Help!" said a boy.

Superhero Max got his magic boots. "Superhero Max can help!" he said.

Activities

The key below describes the skills practiced in each activity.

✏️ Spelling and writing

📖 Reading

💬 Speaking

❓ Critical thinking

✳️ Preparation for the Cambridge Young Learners Exams

1 **Look and read. Match the sentences to the pictures.**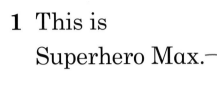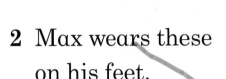

1 This is Superhero Max.

2 Max wears these on his feet.

3 This man stops bad people.

4 This boy robs banks.

5 This woman is Ricky's mother. She robs banks, too.

31

2 Look and read. Write *yes* or *no*.

Max was a boy. He was a superhero, too.

Max had magic boots. He wore the boots and he was Superhero Max!

Superhero Max stopped bad people and he helped good people.

1 Max was a boy. .....yes.....

2 Max was a superhero, too. ....

3 Max had magic shoes. ....

4 Superhero Max stopped all people. ....

5 Superhero Max helped good people. ....

3 Find the words.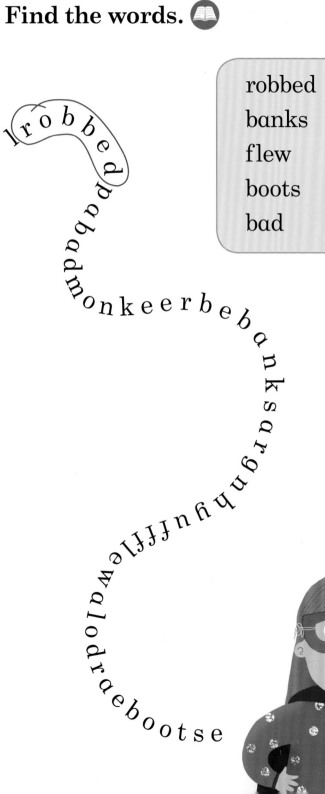

robbed
banks
flew
boots
bad

lrobbedpabadmonkeerbebanksarganhyufffflewalodraebootse

4 **Choose the correct words and write them on the lines.** 📖 ✏️ ⭐

bad   mom   Rob   robbed   robbing

1 Ricky Rob was a _____bad_____ person.

2 He _____ banks.

3 Lady Rob was Ricky's _____.

4 Lady _____ was a bad person, too.

5 She liked _____ banks with Ricky.

5 **Talk about the two pictures with a friend. How are they different? Use the words and phrases below.**

on a bike   frightened   in a town

robbing a bank   bags of money

inside a house   smiling   happy

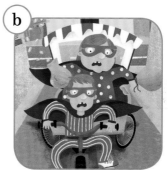

In picture a, Lady Rob is happy.

In picture b, Lady Rob is frightened.

6 Circle the correct words.

1
a magic boots
b magic bank

2
a Ricky Rob
b Superhero Max

3
a Lady Rob
b Ricky Rob

4
a police car
b policeman

7 **Write the correct sentences.**

| was | Max | boy | Superhero | a | . |

1 Superhero Max was a boy.

| had | magic | He | boots | . |

2 ....

| good | helped | Superhero | Max |

| people | . |

3 ....

| people | bad | He | stopped | . |

4 ....

8 **Look at the letters. Write the words.** 📖 ✏️ ✿

oShupeerr

1 A boy ran to ⟶ Superhero ⟵ Max.

pesle

2 "You must not _____," he said.

knab

3 "Lady Rob wants to rob the _____!"

gcima

4 Superhero Max did not have any _____ boots.

38

9 Who says this?

Superhero Max

Lady Rob

policeman

1 "Lady Rob! Stop!" said
Superhero Max .

2 "You cannot fly,
Superhero Max!" said

                                                         .

3 "I can stop the magic boots," said

                                                         .

4 "You cannot rob the
bank again," said

                                                         .

5 "You ARE a superhero!" said the

                                                         .

10 **Read the questions.**
Write complete answers.

Lady Rob and Ricky Rob flew above the houses. They had the money from the bank!

"You cannot stop us, Superhero Max!" they said.

1 Where did Lady Rob and Ricky Rob fly?

They flew above the houses.

2 What did they have?

....

3 What did they say?

" ....

.... !"

11 **Ask and answer the questions with a friend.**

"But I can stop the magic boots," said Superhero Max.

Superhero Max sent magic to the boots. The boots and the bad people flew to a policeman.

1 Did the policeman come?

Yes, he did.

2 Who could stop the magic boots?

3 How were the boots stopped?

4 What happened to the bad people?

12 Look and read. Put a ✓ or a ✗ in the boxes. 📖 ✿

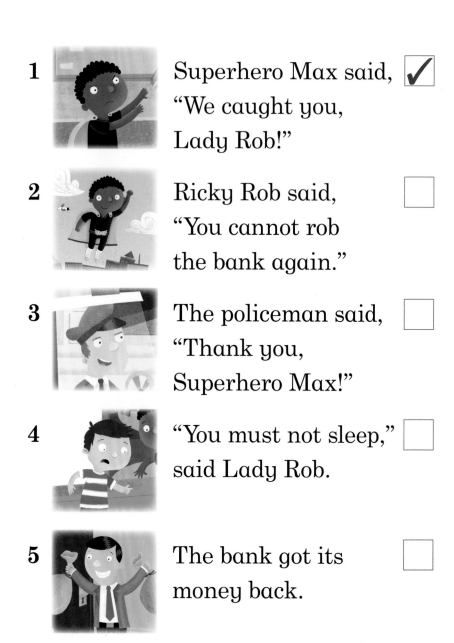

1   Superhero Max said, "We caught you, Lady Rob!"   ✓

2   Ricky Rob said, "You cannot rob the bank again."   ☐

3   The policeman said, "Thank you, Superhero Max!"   ☐

4   "You must not sleep," said Lady Rob.   ☐

5   The bank got its money back.   ☐

13 **Circle the correct words.**

1 (Where)/ **What** did Superhero Max go?

2 **Who** / **Where** said, "Help, Superhero Max!"?

3 **Who** / **What** did Superhero Max do?

4 **Who** / **Where** can help the boy?

5 **Where** / **What** was on the table?

6 **When** / **Where** was the boy?

14 **Look at the letters. Write the words.** 📖 🖊 ⭐

g h t c a u

1 "We ⎯⎯⎯ *caught* ⎯⎯⎯ you,
Lady Rob!" said Superhero Max.

i k c R y

2 "We caught you, ⎯⎯⎯⎯⎯⎯
Rob!"

b o r

3 "You cannot ⎯⎯⎯ the bank again."

o h e r s u e p r

4 "You ARE a ⎯⎯⎯⎯⎯⎯!"
said the policeman.

Order the story. Write 1—5.

.... Lady Rob ran from the bank with all the money.

___1___ "You must not sleep," said the boy. "Lady Rob wants to rob the bank!"

.... Superhero Max sent magic to the boots.

.... The boots and the bad people flew to a policeman.

.... Max could not fly. He ran to the bank.

16 Do the crossword.

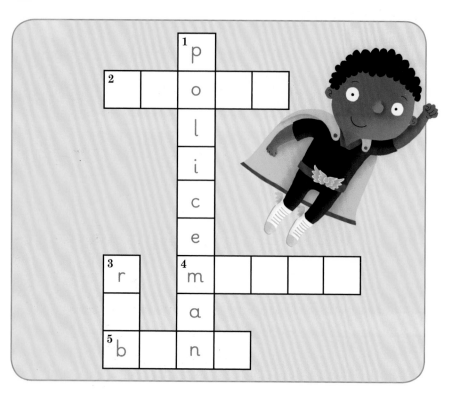

Down

1 This man helps good people and stops bad people.

3 Lady Rob and her son did this.

Across

2 Superhero Max wore these on his feet.

4 Max sent this to the boots.

5 Lady Rob took the money from the . . .

17 **Ask and answer the questions with a friend.** 💬 ❓

1

> *Who were the good people in the story?*

> *Max and the policeman were the good people.*

2 What did the good people do?

3 Were Lady Rob and her son good people or bad people?

4 Where did Lady Rob and Ricky Rob go at the end of the story, do you think?

5 Why did the boy go to Max's house at the end of the story?

Level 2

The Gingerbread Man	**Sly Fox and Red Hen**	**The Monster Next Door**	**Wild Animals**	**Little Red Riding Hood**
978-0-241-25442-4	978-0-241-25443-1	978-0-241-25444-8	978-0-241-25445-5	978-0-241-25446-2
Dinosaurs	**Topsy and Tim The Big Race**	**Goes to the Treehouse**	**Sports Day**	**Going on a Picnic**
978-0-241-25447-9	978-0-241-25448-6	978-0-241-25449-3	978-0-241-26222-1	978-0-241-26221-4
Peter Rabbit and the Angry Owl	**Superhero Max**	**We Can Help!**	**Daddy Pig's New Van**	**School Trip**
978-0-241-28369-1	978-0-241-28368-4	978-0-241-28367-7	978-0-241-28371-4	978-0-241-28372-1

Now you're ready for Level 3!